As Time Whirls Slowly Past

AMY LAURENS

OTHER WORKS

Where Shadows Rise
Through Roads Between
When Worlds Collide

How Not To Acquire A Castle

A Fox of Storms And Starlight

April Showers
Bones Of The Sea
Darkness And Good
Dreaming Of Forests
It All Changes Now
Of Sea Foam And Blood
Rush Job
The Ice Cream Crown Skating Races
Trust Issues

How To Plan A Pinterest-Worthy Party Without Dying
How To Write Dogs
How To Theme
How To Create Cultures
How To Create Life
How To Map
The 32 Worst Mistakes People Make About Dogs

Find other works by the author at www.amylaurens.com

As Time Whirls Slowly Past

INKLET #84

AMY LAURENS

Inkprint
PRESS

www.inkprintpress.com

Print ISBN: 978-1-922434-24-1
eBook ISBN: 9798201514365

www.inkprintpress.com

National Library of Australia Cataloguing-in-Publication Data
Laurens, Amy 1985 –
As Time Whirls Slowly Past
40 p.
ISBN: 978-1-922434-24-1
Inkprint Press, Canberra, Australia
1. Fiction—Family Life—General 2. Fiction—Women 3. Fiction—Short Stories

First Print Edition: June 2022
Cover photo © Serezniy via Deposit Photos
Cover design © Inkprint Press
Interior art © Amy Laurens

AS TIME WHIRLS
SLOWLY PAST

Ashley got the fright of her life
for the third time that day as she
opened the laundry to be confronted
by her daughter's Labrador-sized stuf-
fed-and-wired unicorn.

She sighed, pressed her hand to her
chest, and waited for the adrenalin to
subside.

Bloody hell. Maybe she just needed
to wash it now and be done with it.
She'd put it in here earlier this morning when her daughter Ellie had peed

on it accidentally—'accidentally' was a common word in their house these days—and if she was going to be super honest, she'd been avoiding cleaning it because it seemed all too hard.

A lot of things seemed too hard right now. All she really wanted was a couple of days to herself—maybe a week if she was being greedy—just to rest, recoup, regather. To stop feeling stretched thin, like there were fifty-three too many things on her to-do list every day.

To stop ending every night feeling like a failure.

But then, the kids had had vegetables for dinner—curry, no less—and they'd gotten through most of their school work for the day and no one had shouted or cried during witching hour. Ashley had even managed to convince Ellie to go to sleep without the giant unicorn guarding her bed, a ten-out-of-ten success she'd never been able to pull off yet in the three years Ellie had owned the toy.

Adrenalin calmed, Ashley took a deep breath of laundry-power-scented air and ran a hand through her slightly itchy, slightly oily, dark hair. Man, a long shower would be nice, too. Un-interrupted, for preference, though with Carter up and down for an hour and a half every night these days, who knew how plausible that actually was.

She'd lock herself in the bathroom with her favourite blackberry bubble bar if she didn't know that he'd just sit outside the door and moan and whine until she got out and settled him again.

Ashley closed her eyes and let her-self sag against the doorframe of the laundry, just for a moment. It wasn't defeat, it was regrouping. Just for a second.

And in five more days, Tom would be home. For good, with any luck, this time.

Five more days.

Ashley wound dirty clothes down into the washing machine, loaded it with powder and lavender fabric softener, listened to the music of the beeps as she adjusted the settings, and set the machine whirring.

She left the laundry with a sigh, snagged a glass of pulpy orange juice from the fridge, and collapsed onto the couch in front of the TV.

Medical drama, white-guy movie, news, news, slapstick… Urgh. Netflix it was.

It was a little ritual she went through every night, and she wasn't even quite sure why, because there was never anything on free-to-air that she was interested in, and Netflix was *right there*, but she persisted with it nevertheless. She'd found, in the last twelve months of Tom being gone one week out of every fortnight, that it was the little, thoughtless rituals that kept you sane when everything else felt like it was falling apart.

Ashley picked out the latest period drama, set it playing, and picked up the embroidery she was working on.

Well, 'working on' was generous; she, like most of the rest of the world right now, was attempting to learn a few 'old school' skills while they were all stuck inside for months on end, and her first attempt at embroidering a row of flowers down the side of Ellie's little jeans looked more like a child's scribble—which was fitting, since Ellie's canvas of choice was herself whenever possible. But this latest attempt, a little pair of flowering cacti in a pair of terracotta pots, was actually looking okay. Recognisable, anyway, and the colours made her happy.

Hopefully Ellie would like it.

Upstairs, footsteps creaked floorboards, muffled by worn carpet.

Ashley sighed. "What is it, Carter?"

Silence.

She set in a couple more stitches, working now on the pale pink stars that served for flowers on the cacti.

Creak. Creeeeak.

Ashley sighed again, but ignored the footsteps, focusing on the period drama where two lovers were melting each other with their gazes from across a room. She snorted. Who could have predicted that real life would have taken such a steep turn back toward eighteen-hundreds courtship.

Briefly, she imagined having to date in a situation like this, when you couldn't even visit someone's house, couldn't really go out in public properly, couldn't eat out or go to the movies or do anything typically date-ish.

Man. Dating was hard enough.

She blinked, shook her head, and refocused on her stitching. After ten years of marriage, that stage was *long* behind her. Thank God.

Creeeeak.

"Mummy…"

Her jaw twitched. "Yes, Carter?"

"I can't get to sleep."

"I know, sweetie. That's normal right now, remember?"

A protracted pause. She never quite knew if that was because he was processing what she'd said or just that he was finally getting sleepy; he didn't tend to do it in the day time.

"Yeah."

The period drama's end-credit music trilled, overcut with a montage of scenes, shots of the main couple staring at each other across rooms, across gardens, staring longingly out of carriage windows at each other.

Ashley might not know what dating from a distance felt like, but she sure knew what marriage-at-a-distance did. She closed her eyes for a second, caught by momentary longing for her husband's arms around her. She tried to make herself believe that she could smell his aftershave, a little sharp, like mint, but soft like lotus and sandalwood too.

"Can I have a shower?"

That was Carter again.

Patience, Ashley reminded herself, *is a virtue*. "Yes, sweetheart. I'll come get you in a bit."

Upstairs, the sound of the hot water pipes screeched a little before settling into their steady, thrumming rhythm.

Chocolate would make everything better.

Ashley tucked her needle into the soft denim of Ellie's jeans and set the jeans aside on the couch. In the kitchen, hidden behind the bright red toaster, was the kids' stash of Easter eggs. If she took a small one from each bucket, they couldn't complain about her being unfair…

She took a gold one from Carter's stash and a pink one from Ellie's, the foil slightly crinkled and gleaming brightly under the kitchen downlights. The foil went into the collection in the otherwise-empty fruit bowl—she'd heard somewhere recently that it could only be recycled in fist-sized balls, so they were clumping it all together as they collectively ate their way through the Easter harvest—and Ashley slumped back on the couch, tossing her feet up over the arm and twisting sideways, one arm lolloping over the side, fingers dragging on the cold tiles of the living room floor.

Which, by the by, was filthy, and she'd probably contaminated herself now with chocolate crumbs or toast crumbs or spilled milk or heck, even pee, who knew.

The tiles were long overdue for a mop. Probably, she should do that before Tom got home. He'd appreciate it, she knew… But he also wouldn't judge her if she didn't do it.

The kids ate vegetables, she reminded herself. *We walked around the pond twice. They only had two hours of iPad time today, a serious improvement on yesterday's seven hours apiece.*

The shower shushed away overhead.

With another sigh—it seemed to be the only way she got any air, some evenings—Ashley hit pause on the TV, licked the last of the chocolate egg from the inside of her cheek, and headed upstairs to fish Carter out of the shower.

The bathroom was steamy and warm, a pleasant contrast to the cool evening downstairs. The smell of soap filled the air… and puddles covered the floor.

And the toilet.

And the carpet outside the bathroom, where child-sized wet footprints told the story of Carter going in to his sister's room to check on her before returning to his shower.

Ashley slumped, but grabbed a white towel from the linen press, wiped up the worst of the water, and rapped her knuckles on the shower's glass door.

Carter's broad, tanned face appeared through a hole he'd rubbed in the steam on the shower door.

"Time to hop out," Ashley said, holding up the towel.

Carter's face disappeared and the water shut off in the shower. The door creaked open and Ashley swaddled him a towel big enough to wrap right around him twice. Seven years old, and he weighed barely any more than his four-year-old sister. Kid was all skin and bones—and muscle, she reminded herself as she towelled him down. He'd been doing gymnastics since he was five, the local club had scouted him at school, and he'd had a six-pack about that long to go with it.

She shook her head, lips pressed to hide a smile. "Love you, kiddo," she said as she finished drying him down and folded the towel neatly in half length-wise.

Carter disappeared off to his bedroom to dress, and Ashley a moment to savour the warm, damp, soapy air, straightening the bath mat, hanging the towel, moving a stray bar of soap that had dried to the counter back to the soap holder over the bath.

"Mum." Carter reappeared in the doorway again, buttoning the shirt of his blue Transformers pyjamas. "Can I leave my light on?"

Valiantly, Ashley resisted the temptation to rub at her forehead. "Sure, kiddo." She couldn't keep the resignation out of her voice, though. "Why not."

She'd fought that one in the beginning, not wanting him to grow reliant on it. But she'd been terrified of the dark as a kid—she still remembered the time that the natural movement in her vision in the dark had seemed like a green, ugly witch's face taunting her from her bookshelves—and the alternative was either a prolonged fight, or her sitting up at the desk on the landing until he fell asleep.

Some nights, that wasn't a terrible proposition either; although the whole difficulty-with-bedtime thing drove her nuts, on another level she couldn't forget feeling exactly the same way when he'd been a toddler learning to settle himself at night as well, and how many hours she'd wasted lying on his floor teaching him to sleep—wasted because of her attitude, her frustration.

Those years had passed, and these would too, probably when the world finally went out of lockdown, whenever that might be.

In the meantime, it seemed prudent all round to avoid as many fights as possible.

She could train him out of using a light to fall asleep some other time, when the world *wasn't* falling apart around them.

"Mummy…"

Patience patience patience patience. "Yes, Carter?"

"I feel like there's something in my room."

Ashley couldn't help herself: she sighed again. "Hold on." She flicked off the heat lamp and the light bulb in the bathroom, went to close the door but changed her mind—keep it open, let it dry out—and crossed the tiny space that wasn't quite small enough to be a hallway but wasn't really big enough to be anything more than a landing for the stairs into Carter's room. "What's up?"

"I feel like there's something under my bed," he said, curled up in a ball, dwarfed in the queen-sized bed he'd inherited when Ashley and Tom had upgraded to a king. Carter peered up at her with big, brown eyes, pitiful and underscored by heavy dark circles.

"Kiddo," Ashley said, running her hand over his head, "you'd really feel a lot better if you could just go to sleep."

And she would feel better with her husband home, and time off from single-parenting, and enough energy to do everything she felt like she needed to do in a day to keep the household running.

Might as well point out how much better they'd all feel if Ellie's toy unicorn came to life and granted them all some wishes.

Momentarily distracted by the hypothetical question of whether or not unicorns could grant wishes, or whether that was something exclusive to genies or jinn, Ashley got down on her knees and peered under the bed.

Dust bunnies, more dust bunnies, a couple big enough to be dust hares, a slew of unpaired socks, a small stack of comic books, and a few pieces of lego.

"There's nothing under there, Carter."

He nodded solemnly, but his expression didn't change.

Ashley thought longingly of her embroidery downstairs, her period drama, her hour and a half of alone time before she'd crash exhausted into bed.

The world wouldn't be like this forever.

And she wouldn't have the kids forever either.

With one last sigh, Ashley flicked off the light.

"What are you doing?" Carter squeaked in alarm.

"Move over," Ashley said. "I'll lie down with you for a bit."

A pause, that protracted silence again, though this time he was also moving over as he thought, making room for her amid the small horde of pillows and stuffed animals he hadn't particularly cared for until he'd acquired a baby sister who loved anything animal more than almost everything else in the world.

"Will you stay until I fall asleep?"

Dim light filtered in from the stairwell, and as she lay down, Ashley noted that Carter's blinds hadn't been drawn all the way down; a sliver of night sky showed, a few stars glimmering way out there beyond. Cold air diffused into the room from the crack, and for a moment she reached to close the blind…

But stars, like children, were something she never quite had the time to appreciate enough.

So she tucked Carter down in his blankets, pulled the uppermost one over her as well, draped her arm around the top of Carter's pillow so it rested against his fuzzy, warm head, and watched as the stars whirled slowly past beyond the silhouette of Carter's perfect, child-like face.

THE MAKING OF
AS TIME WHIRLS SLOWLY PAST

This is a story close to my heart, because although it isn't *true*, it's a very *near* truth. My daughter did, in fact, have such a unicorn as the one in this story (and the illustration!), and it did, in fact, give me a near heart-attack one night when I came across it in the laundry.

My son does, in fact, share that tendency of coming out to comment on—well, whatever—just as he's very nearly falling asleep.

And for an extended period of our lives while the children were little, my spouse was out of town for three or four days every fortnight. It was draining, and exhausting in the way that parenting small children simply is, but one night I sat down and wrote this story—in April of 2020 it was, during our first Covid-19 lockdown, for a challenge I'd set myself to write 10 stories in 20 days—and when I reached the ending, it was like an epiphany.

The lesson our main character learns here is a lesson I learned right along with her as I wrote it: Slow down. Enjoy what you have while you have it. This too shall pass, and often sooner than you'd expect. There is joy to be found in every season, even if the joy is only small, and mundane, and even if from another angle it didn't look like joy at all.

It was a lesson I needed to learn— and one I'm still learning, as I try to retrain my brain to pause, to drink life in, and to stop rushing in a high-strung, stressed-out fashion from one project constantly to the next.

Read more by Amy Laurens!

CRYSTALLINE AND BRIGHT

I stood, staring down into the teal-blue river water, ignoring the chatter behind my back. The snow covered the ground around me, hiding bumps and ridges, soothing out sharp edges. To my right, the dark stone shadow of the bridge stood like a guardian, watchful, alert. Snow rimmed its edges; every so often some shifted in a sudden breeze and landed in the quiet river below with a gentle splash.

The willows on the far bank slept quietly under their snow blanket, their green sappy smell hidden by the cold, sharp scent of the snow.

Stop.

Start again.

It wasn't actually winter. It was early spring, with the grass green and new, the sound of a lawnmower buzzing in the distance and the scent of cut grass drifting on the wind. Moss covered the shadowed side of the old stone bridge, and willows stretched their fingers to the slow-moving, drowsy little river that bordered the grounds of the school.

A butterfly flittered past, white wings speckled with black like soot.

The world felt fresh, and green, and full of promise.

I was still ignoring the chattering behind me.

Stop.

Start again.

It's summer, and the air is swelteringly hot. Sweat drips down the back of my neck, pools under my arms, under my awkward breasts. The river in front of me is milky-blue, gentle, quiet, and I long to strip off my shirt and jeans and throw myself into the water.

It's not just the breathtakingly sharp cold of the icemelt I'm craving; it's the feeling of being *clean*.

The air stinks of a fish that Lander left out on the bank near the bridge, rotting to pieces in the high temperatures.

I'm still ignoring the chatter.

Stop.

Let's try once more.

It's autumn—of course—and the willows have turned yellow, their little leaves dropping into the milk-water, eddying slowly away from the shadow of the bridge.

Behind me, the emerald lawn of the old school buildings is ringed with gem-toned maples, butter-leafed poplars, silver-and-gold birches. Occasionally, the wind catches stray leaves and flings them into the pond.

I can still hear the voices behind me.

All of these pictures are true, and none of them are.

Not precisely, not uniquely; they're all composites, the merging and piecing together of hundreds of memories of similar experiences, of all the times I stood on the river bank and stared longingly into its depths, imagining myself a naiad with a secret home to return to, somewhere people loved me.

These images have to be composites, because for every time I was down at the river, I was focusing only on two things: ignoring the voices, and watching the water.

All the other details, the little bits of specificity that allow me to recall the place in so much explicit detail? I never noticed them at the time.

And so I have to piece them together, collage-fashion, or else I have nothing to say. Nothing to see.

Nothing except the water, milky-blue that occasionally, in the right light, at the right time of day, flashed teal and came alive.

I'd lived with the voices as long as I could remember. Some of them were real, inasmuch as they belonged to real, live people whom other people could see, who grew and developed and changed with the passing of the seasons; some of them were *sur*real, inasmuch as they belonged to people I could see, but that none other could, and who did not change or grow with the passing of the seasons.

And some of the voices... Some of them I could never divine exactly what they were.

But all of them, real, surreal and unknown, had one thing in common: none of them liked me.

I could never figure out why. Oh, sure, I came to the school without the name and pedigree of any of the other students, a supposed-orphan with no memory of her life before double digits and no connections to speak of. I wasn't part of their circle, my excellent trust fund notwithstanding, and so the real people, the live people, couldn't accept me.

It shouldn't have been that way. It seemed to me that I hadn't done anything wrong, or untoward, hadn't neglected to do anything needed, hadn't slighted or snubbed any who hadn't already done so several times to me.

And yet, for all the years I was there at the school, its grand, lofty double-storey buildings made from pale stone like a castle, ivy creeping all about like Christmas lights, the lawn constantly emerald, the hedges consistently clipped... For all those composite years, no one ever liked me.

Well, a slight exaggeration: my teachers liked me well enough. I was a diligent student.

And the river liked me. I could tell that, because when I was close to the river, the other voices kept their distance—and the river had a voice of its own. And once or twice, I could have sworn it also had a face.

Keep reading! Head to www.inkprintpress.com/ amylaurens/aprilshowers/ to buy your copy now!

ABOUT THE AUTHOR

AMY LAURENS is an Australian author of fantasy fiction for all ages.

Amy has written the award-winning portal-fantasy *Sanctuary* series about Edge, a 13-year-old girl forced to move to a small country town because of witness protection (the first book is *Where Shadows Rise*), the humorous fantasy *Kaditeos* series, following newly graduated Evil Overlord Mercury as she attempts to acquire a castle, the young adult series *Storm Foxes* about love and magic and family in small town Australia, and a whole host of non-fiction and shorter works.

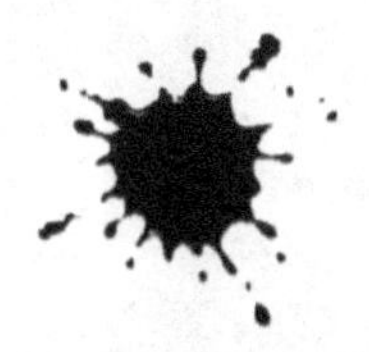

INKLETS

Collect them all! Released on the 1st and 15th of each month.

Shadows NEVER LIE
AMY LAURENS
Here She Lies
LIANA BROOKS
Perfect Destruction
An Age Of Unicorns Story
AMY LAURENS
What Blood Can Do
AMY LAURENS
Dancer, Dreamer Seer
LIANA BROOKS
As Time Whirls Slowly Past
AMY LAURENS
Far More Satisfying Than Hell
AMY LAURENS
Just Another Day In Hell
LIANA BROOKS
Moon AND Morning
AMY LAURENS

Some
Impropriety
Expected
AMY LAURENS

NEON SNOW
LIANA BROOKS

Reincarnation
LIANA BROOKS

More Than
Mushrooms
AMY LAURENS

DOUBLE ISSUE
How To Make A Star
& The World Ended
LIANA BROOKS

CAUGHT
IN THE ACT
AMY LAURENS

ANUBIS
Has Sent You
Six Souls
LIANA BROOKS

PRAYER TO A
GODDESS
LIANA BROOKS

Love In The
Time Of Corona
AMY LAURENS

www.ingramcontent.com/pod-product-compliance
Lightning Source LLC
Chambersburg PA
CBHW030813190726

48285CB00003B/1161